Humphrey's

Playful Puppy Problem

Look for more of

HUMPHREY'S TINY TALES

Humphrey's Really Wheely Racing Day

Humphrey's
Playful Puppy Problem

Betty G. Birney

illustrated by **Priscilla Burris**

G. P. PUTNAM'S SONS
An Imprint of Penguin Group (USA)
Park School Campus
400 W. Townline Road
Round Lake, IL 60073

G. P. PUTNAM'S SONS
Published by the Penguin Group
Penguin Group (USA) LLC
375 Hudson Street, New York, NY 10014

USA | Canada | UK | Ireland | Australia
New Zealand | India | South Africa | China
penguin.com
A Penguin Random House Company

Library of Congress Cataloging-in-Publication Data
Birney, Betty G.
Humphrey's playful puppy problem / Betty G. Birney ; illustrated by
Priscilla Burris.
pages cm.—(Humphrey's tiny tales)
Summary: Humphrey, the pet hamster of Classroom 26, is helping Richie
with a science project, but Richie's feisty puppy gets in the way.
[1. Hamsters—Fiction. 2. Science projects—Fiction. 3. Dogs—Fiction.
4. Animals—Infancy—Fiction. 5. Schools—Fiction.] I. Burris, Priscilla,
illustrator. II. Title.
PZ7.B5229Ht 2014
[Fic]—dc23
2013028265

Printed in the United States of America.
ISBN 978-0-399-25202-0
3 5 7 9 10 8 6 4 2

Design by Ryan Thomann.
Text set in ITC Stone Informal Std Medium.

To Rebecca and Gary Frank
—B.B.

For Susan, Cecilia, and Ryan—
Gratefully!
—P.B.

Contents

Pet Project

It was Friday afternoon at Longfellow School. I'm the classroom hamster in Room 26.

I was nibbling on a yummy carrot stick when I heard Mrs. Brisbane say, "Class, don't forget to bring in your science projects on Monday."

That was such exciting news, I almost dropped my carrot.

My classmates had been talking about their experiments all week. They sounded very interesting!

I turned to Og, the other classroom pet. "Did you hear that, Og?" I said. "We're going to see all of the science projects on Monday!"

"BOING! BOING!" Og replied. He makes a funny sound, but he can't help it. He's a frog.

"Would any of you like to tell us about your project now?" Mrs. Brisbane asked.

"I would!" Raise-Your-Hand-Heidi called out.

"Heidi, what did you forget to do?" Mrs. Brisbane said.

Heidi raised her hand. "Sorry," she said. "I'm testing different liquids to see how long it takes for them to freeze."

"Interesting," Mrs. Brisbane said. "What have you tried?"

"Plain water, sugar water and salt water," Heidi said.

A.J.'s hand shot up. "I don't get it," he said in his loud voice. "Won't they be melted by the time you get to school?"

"Lower your voice, A.J.," Mrs. Brisbane reminded him.

"All right," he said in a softer voice. "But won't they melt?"

"Yes," Heidi said. "So I'm taking pictures and keeping a chart. That's what I'll bring in."

Just thinking about things that are COLD-COLD-COLD made me shiver, even though I have a fur coat!

"How about you, Sayeh?" Mrs. Brisbane asked next. Speak-Up-Sayeh didn't raise her hand because she doesn't like to talk in class.

Sayeh smiled shyly. "I'm growing beans on my windowsill," she said. "Some will have full sun and some will be covered."

Stop-Giggling-Gail was growing mold in her refrigerator.

6

Mold sounded yucky, but Gail
said it was fun.

Pay-Attention-Art
talked about magnets
and Golden-Miranda
said something
about making
a rainbow.

Then I noticed
Richie Rinaldi waving
his hand.

Mrs. Brisbane asked
him to speak.

He said something like
"Smytrm-hum-hum." At least

7

that's what *I* heard. And hamsters have very good hearing.

"Repeat it please, Richie," Mrs. Brisbane said. "And this time, say it so I can understand it."

"It's my turn to take Humphrey home this weekend—right?" Richie asked. "I need him for my experiment."

I was happy to hear that. Classroom pets like me *love* to be needed.

"I thought your project was about ants," Mrs. Brisbane said.

"It was," Richie replied. "But my mom didn't like having ants in the house. Now I have a better idea using a hamster."

Mrs. Brisbane checked her list. "Yes, Richie," she said. "It's your turn to take Humphrey home. Do you want to tell us about your new experiment?"

"Yes, tell us!" I shouted.

Of course, all my friends heard was SQUEAK-SQUEAK-SQUEAK.

Richie thought for a moment. "I think it should be a surprise."

Kirk Chen raised his hand. "I know what it is," he said. "Richie's going to turn Humphrey into a monster!"

Then he raised his arms straight out in front of him and made a scary face.

"And when he's a monster, he can have a *ghoul friend!*" Kirk added.

Everybody laughed.

It was funny, unless you were the hamster who was going to be turned into a monster!

And I really didn't want a ghoul friend!

"BOING-BOING-BOING-BOING!" Og sounded worried.

After all, his tank sits next to my cage on the table by the window.

He probably didn't want to have a monster for a neighbor.

But Richie had a big smile on his face.

I was happy for him.

I would have been even happier if I'd known what the experiment was going to be!

～～～

When we were on the school bus that afternoon, Richie told me, "I have a surprise for you at home."

The bus was bumpy and thumpy. I slid from one side of my cage to the other.

"Just you wait," Richie said. "It's a giant surprise."

A giant is something like a monster. Did Richie already have a giant at home?

"Eeek!" I squeaked.

Richie just laughed. "You'll find out soon enough," he said.

The surprise had a name: Poppy.

Poppy was a puppy.

She was small, with curly black fur, and she *loved* to bark.

All that barking made my ears twitch and my whiskers wiggle.

"Isn't she great, Humphrey?" Richie asked. He set my cage on the desk in his room. "I've wanted a dog for years and finally my parents let me have one."

I didn't really think Poppy was great.

I don't think *any* dog is great.

Dogs have large, pointed teeth and wet noses. They have big tails and sharp claws.

And they aren't usually friendly to small creatures like me.

"Woof!" Poppy barked. She tried to jump up and see me.

Luckily, she was too short to get all the way up to my cage.

"She likes you, Humphrey." Richie laughed. "She wants to be your friend."

"Woof!" Poppy barked. She even wagged her tail.

But I still didn't think she wanted to be my friend.

"Wait until Uncle Aldo comes over tomorrow," Richie said. "He's going to help me with my experiment."

Richie's Uncle Aldo is also our school's custodian.

At night, when he comes into Room 26 to clean, he talks to Og and me. Sometimes he balances a broom on one finger and gives us treats.

I was glad I would be seeing Aldo the next day.

I wasn't glad about the experiment, though.

After dinner, it was time to watch a movie. Richie put my cage on a shelf in the living room. Poppy couldn't jump that high, but that didn't stop her from trying.

She looked up at me and barked and barked and barked some more.

"WOOF-WOOF! WOOF-WOOF! WOOF-WOOF!"

Richie's mom finally put the

puppy in the
kitchen so we could start
the movie.

It was about a mad scientist
named Frankenstein who created
a scary monster.

He hooked him up to a scary machine. There was lightning . . . and the monster came to life. He had a flat head and bolts sticking out of his neck.

The sight of him made my fur stand up on end!

Richie came over to my cage. He made weird faces at me and said "Humphrey-stein" in a creepy voice. Then he laughed. "Mwa-ha-ha!"

He didn't sound like Richie at all.

By the time Richie brought me into his room and went to bed, it was raining outside.

Would there be lightning?

Would I end up with bolts in my neck, like Dr. Frankenstein's monster?

Would people call me "Humphrey-stein"?

I crawled into my little sleeping house but I didn't sleep a wink.

I LOVE-LOVE-LOVE being a hamster.

But I would *not* love to be a monster.

I Go for a Spin

During the week, I get to see Aldo every night. I hardly ever get to see him outside of school.

So I was HAPPY-HAPPY-HAPPY when he came into Richie's room on Saturday afternoon.

"Greetings,
my fine
furry friend,"
Aldo said.

"Glad to see you, Aldo!" I squeaked back.

He laughed. "I think you're glad to see me, too."

I love to make Aldo laugh. When he does, his big, furry mustache shakes so hard, I sometimes think it's going to fall off.

"I hear Richie has planned an experiment with you," Aldo said.

I wouldn't mind if Richie did an experiment *with* me. I just wouldn't want him to do an experiment *on* me.

"Thanks for helping me, Uncle Aldo," Richie said.

Just then, Poppy came racing into Richie's room. She ran in a circle around Aldo's feet.

"Poppy, no!" Aldo said in a firm voice. "Sit."

Poppy did not sit. Instead, she jumped up and put her front paws on Aldo's legs.

Then Poppy noticed me. She raced up to the desk and looked straight at me.

"WOOF-WOOF!" she barked.

"Go away!" I squeaked.

My squeaking only made Poppy bark more.

"Look!" Richie said. "Poppy wants to play with Humphrey."

The thought of Poppy playing with me made me shiver and quiver.

Poppy kept on barking. "WOOF-WOOF-WOOF!"

Her voice was so loud, it made my tiny hamster ears hurt!

"Time for you to go," Aldo said. He picked up the little dog and carried her out of the room.

Then he came back in without
Poppy and closed the door. "Now
we can get to work," he said.

"THANKS-THANKS-THANKS,
Aldo!" I squeaked.

Aldo said, "I think Humphrey
is glad that Poppy's outside."

Aldo is a very smart human!

Richie and Aldo pulled chairs
up to the desk and looked into
my cage.

"HI-HI-HI!" I squeaked.

"So, what you want to do?"
Aldo asked Richie.

I scrambled to the front of my cage so I could hear Richie's plan.

"I want to see how many times Humphrey can spin his wheel in three minutes," Richie said.

I love spinning on my wheel, so that sounded GREAT-GREAT-GREAT to me.

"That's a good idea," Aldo said. "How are you going to do that?"

Richie shrugged. "I'm not sure. He spins pretty fast. Don't you, Humphrey?"

I scampered over to my wheel
and began to spin.

"Hey! Humphrey must have
understood you," Aldo said.

"But that's impossible," Richie
replied. "He's a hamster."

Aldo laughed. "You never know with Humphrey."

They both leaned in closer as I began to spin faster and faster.

"I see the problem," Aldo said. "He spins so fast, it's hard to count how many times the wheel goes around."

"Yes," Richie agreed. "Should I tell him to slow down?"

Aldo shook his head. "No. Then it wouldn't be a real experiment."

I kept on spinning while Richie and Aldo thought about the problem.

Then I heard a distant "WOOF-WOOF!" Poppy was scratching at the door and barking.

"Go away, Poppy!" Richie yelled.

I don't think Poppy could hear him over all that barking.

She made me so jumpy, I spun the wheel faster and faster.

"Look at Humphrey go,"

Richie said.

"I wish Poppy would go," I squeaked. "I wish she'd go far, far away!"

Aldo and Richie watched me spin on the wheel.

"You need a way to mark each time the wheel goes around once," Aldo said.

I kept spinning and they kept

thinking. I was hoping they had an idea soon, because to squeak the truth, I was getting tired.

"I know," Aldo said. "We need something that makes a sound."

Whew! I was GLAD-GLAD-GLAD that Aldo had had an idea.

I let my wheel slow down a bit while I tried to think of something that makes a sound.

I looked over at the side of the cage where my water bottle and food dish are. Sometimes my water bottle makes a GLUG-

GLUG-GLUG sound, but it's not very loud.

I looked over at my poo corner—no sound there!

I looked down at my soft bedding. It was nice and quiet.

Then I looked up and saw a tiny little bell. Not long ago, my friends gave it to me for a surprise.

I stopped spinning and hopped off my wheel.

Then I scampered up to the top of my cage and rang the little bell with my paw.

DING-
DING-DING!

Aldo and Richie were so busy
thinking, they didn't hear it.

I tried again. DING-DING-
DING-DING!

36

This time, Aldo looked up. "What's that sound?" he asked.

Richie looked up, too. "Oh, that's Humphrey's new bell," he said.

Aldo leaned in close to my cage. "A bell? That's just what we need! Thanks, Humphrey!"

"You're welcome," I told him. Aldo probably didn't understand my squeaks, but I was happy he liked my idea.

Richie and Aldo got to work. First, Richie took my wheel out of the cage and put it on the desk.

"Don't worry, Humphrey," he said. "You'll get it back."

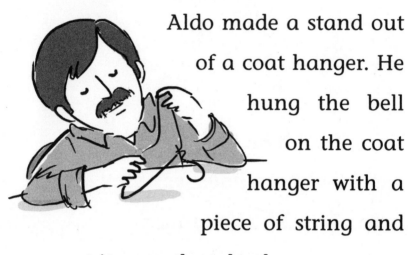

Aldo made a stand out of a coat hanger. He hung the bell on the coat hanger with a piece of string and set it near the wheel.

"We need something that will ring the bell each time the wheel spins," Aldo said. "It must be strong enough to ring the bell but small enough to fit under the wheel."

This time, Richie came up with a good idea.

Soon, they had attached a bent paper clip to the side of my wheel.

"Humphrey, we need your help again," Richie said.

That was GOOD-GOOD-GOOD news, because classroom hamsters love to help!

Richie reached into my cage and gently placed me on my wheel again. "You know what to do, Humphrey," he said.

Yes, I did!

I began to spin my wheel, faster and faster.

DING-DING-DING-DING-DING!

Just then, Richie put his hand on my wheel. I stopped so suddenly, I tumbled over.

"Sorry, Humphrey," he said.

As he gently placed me back in my cage, Richie told me, "I need to finish the rest of the experiment."

The *rest* of the experiment? What was coming next?

Would I end up like the monster in the Frankenstein movie?

Just then, I heard something whining and scratching at the door.

Poppy was back!

"WOOF-WOOF!" she barked.

I shivered a little.

I didn't want to turn into a monster.

And I REALLY-REALLY-REALLY didn't want to play with Poppy!

The Great
Dog Disaster

Aldo opened the door and picked
Poppy up. "Come on, pup. I think
we need some peace and quiet."

I know I did!

He took her out the door.

Richie quietly drew a chart and

began decorating a big board describing his experiment.

"Poppy loves fetching that ball," Aldo said when he came back. "I left her outside for a while."

That was GOOD-GOOD-GOOD news!

Aldo gave Richie a stopwatch so he could time my spinning.

"Are you ready, Humphrey?" Richie asked.

He gently took me out of my cage and set me on the wheel.

I started spinning, slowly at first. Then I picked up speed.

"Ready, set, go!" Richie said as he started the stopwatch.

I spun faster and faster.

DING-DING!

Each time the bell rang, Richie made a mark on his chart.

DING-DING-DING!

I picked up speed.

"Go, Humphrey!" Aldo said.

DING-DING-DING-DING!

I spun so fast, Richie had trouble keeping up.

"That's one minute," Richie said. "Keep going, Humphrey."

I can spin on my wheel for a long time. And I liked the sound of the bell ringing.

Aldo took pictures of me.

"Smile, Humphrey!" he said as a bright light flashed.

"That's two minutes," Richie announced.

I kept on spinning and spinning. After all, I wanted Richie to get good grades for his experiment.

I lost track of how many minutes I spun.

"That's good," Richie said after a while. "You can rest now, Humphrey."

He slowed the wheel with his hand and then moved me back to my cage.

"I think Humphrey needs a nap," Aldo said.

He was right about that!

"And I have to get home," Aldo added. "I don't think you need my help anymore."

Richie said good-bye and sat down at his desk to write his report.

I burrowed under my soft bedding and fell asleep.

~

Later, when Richie got into bed, his mom and dad came in to say good night.

"Will you be able to finish the project tomorrow?" his dad asked.

"Yes," Richie said with a smile. "I'm almost finished now."

When they left the room, his parents turned out the lights and shut the door.

But it wasn't long before I heard someone scratching and whining outside.

It was Poppy!

"Sometimes she sleeps in my room, Humphrey," Richie said.

"But I think I should keep her away from you."

"*Far* away!" I agreed.

Luckily, I heard Richie's mom say, "No, Poppy. You'll sleep in our room tonight."

And then, finally, it was quiet.

I slept well that night and so did Richie.

~~~~~

On Sunday afternoon, Richie worked on his project.

Once in a while, I'd hear Poppy scratching at the door. Sometimes, she even barked. "WOOF-WOOF!"

But Richie kept the door tightly closed, which made me happy!

I had to do some more spinning for Richie. I got a little tired, but he said I did a great job.

By late afternoon, the report, a chart and the photos were attached to a big board. My wheel with the paper clip and the stand with the bell sat next to it.

Richie had used bright colors

and it looked GREAT-GREAT-GREAT!

"You did a hamster-iffic job!" I squeaked to Richie.

"It turned out pretty well," Richie said. "I just hope Mrs. Brisbane likes it."

"She will!" I told him.

~~~~~

Richie's whole family came in to see his experiment.

Richie put me on the wheel and I started spinning as fast as

I could while he explained how it
worked.

His two sisters and his brother
were so excited to see me spin, I
went even faster.

"Go, Humphrey, go!"
they shouted.

When Richie made me stop spinning, his mom said, "I'm proud of you, Richie."

"I'm proud of you *and* Humphrey," his dad said. "Let's celebrate and go out for supper."

"Sounds like fun!" I squeaked.

But it turns out that hamsters aren't allowed in restaurants. Not even neat and polite hamsters like me.

Soon, I was alone in Richie's room. The house was quiet and I dozed off.

I'm not sure how long I was asleep before I heard a whining sound.

Poppy was outside Richie's bedroom door!

Luckily the door was shut.

I closed my eyes and tried to get back to sleep. Then I heard a scratching sound.

"WOOF-WOOF!" Poppy barked.

The noise got louder and louder and the door began to shake.

I'm not sure what Poppy did, but suddenly, the door burst open and there she was!

She ran straight toward the desk, jumped up on Richie's chair and looked at me.

I have never been so happy to live in a cage!

But if Poppy could open the door to the room, could she also open the door to my cage?

She might figure out that my cage has a lock-that-doesn't-lock.

My heart was pounding.

"Stay away!" I squeaked. "I don't want to play."

"WOOF-WOOF," she answered, wagging her tail. Poppy put her front legs up on the top of the desk to try to get closer.

Suddenly there was a loud crash as her floppy puppy paws sent the wheel sliding across the desk.

The big board collapsed and

the bell went DING-DING-DING-DING.

Luckily, the noise scared Poppy. She jumped off the chair and ran out of the room.

I was HAPPY-HAPPY-HAPPY that she was gone.

But I was SORRY-SORRY-SORRY when I looked at the desk.

The pieces of Richie's project were scattered everywhere. It was completely ruined!

All because of that playful puppy.

"Oh, no!"

Richie shouted when he returned.

His mom and dad ran into the room.

"What could have happened?" Mrs. Rinaldi said.

Mr. Rinaldi looked around the room.

"Richie, was the door open when you got back?" he asked. "Because I remember closing it before we left so Poppy couldn't get in."

"Yes, it was," Richie said. "So I guess she must have done it."

"YES-YES-YES!" I squeaked. "Poppy came in and wrecked the project!"

Richie sat down and tried to fix the project.

The board was torn, so Richie taped it back together. He smoothed out his wrinkled report.

"Where's the bell?" Richie asked.

His dad began to search for it.

"And where's the paper clip?" Richie wondered.

"It slid under the lamp!" I shouted. "And the bell is under the desk." They couldn't understand me, but they did find the bell.

"We have to find all of the pieces," Richie said. "The project is due tomorrow!"

Finally, Mrs. Rinaldi lifted the lamp. "Here's the paper clip," she said.

I felt a lot better and so did Richie.

But when he got the project back together, it didn't work.

He put me on the wheel and I began to spin.

When the paper clip hit the bell, the bell fell off.

He worked on it some more. This time, when the paper clip hit the bell, the clip fell off.

"Oh, I can't do anything right," Richie said.

Richie's dad tried to help. When he finished, the bell didn't fall off, but it didn't ring at all. It went "CLUNK."

"Richie needs to get to bed," Mrs. Rinaldi said. "Now."

"I'm sure you can fix it in the morning, son," Mr. Rinaldi said. "We all need some sleep."

I know Richie didn't want to go to bed, but soon he was fast asleep.

I, however, was wide awake.

The moon glowed brightly and I could see the wheel from my cage. I stared and stared at it all night long.

It was almost morning when I finally saw the problem.

Mr. Rinaldi had fastened the bell too tightly. Someone needed to loosen the string so the bell would swing freely. Then it would ring again.

And I was the only someone who knew what to do.

The Playful
Puppy Returns

The room was already getting light, so I knew there was no time to waste!

I jiggled the lock-that-doesn't-lock on my cage. The door swung open.

I was about to scurry over to the wheel to repair the bell, when Richie's mom knocked on the door.

"Richie! Time to get up!" she called out.

I hurried back to my cage as fast as my small legs would carry me.

After all, if I ever get caught outside of my cage, someone might fix my lock-that-doesn't-lock. Then, I could never get out and help my friends again.

Just as I closed the door, Richie jumped out of bed.

He yawned and said, "Hi, Humphrey."

"Good morning," I squeaked back politely.

He came over to look at the wheel. "I wish I could get that bell to ring," he said.

His mom called from the hall.

"Come and have your breakfast, Richie. You're going to be late!"

"But I need to fix my project," he replied.

"You have to eat first," she said.

Richie sighed and left his room.

I knew if he was eating breakfast, he'd be gone for a while. I opened the door to my cage again and hurried over to the wheel.

It wouldn't take long for me to loosen the string so the bell would ring.

Suddenly, I heard the pitter-patter of paws on the floor. I looked up and saw that Richie had left the door open.

Poppy was heading straight toward me!

"Go away, Poppy!" I squeaked.

She hopped up on the chair and stared at me across the desk.

I could see her shiny teeth, and this time I didn't have my cozy cage to protect me.

I glanced around and saw a pile of paper clips on the desk.

I threw a few of them at her
nose, hoping to scare her away.

Poppy growled, but she didn't
move.

Then I remembered that Aldo

had said she liked playing with a
ball. I'd seen a little bouncy ball
on Richie's desk.

I scurried to it and rolled it
toward the edge.

"Here, Poppy—go fetch the ball!" I squeaked.

The ball rolled off the side of the desk and across the floor.

While the pup chased after it, I worked on loosening the string.

To my surprise, Poppy came right back with the ball in her mouth.

She hopped up on the chair and set the ball on the desk.

"WOOF-WOOF!" she barked.

Poppy still wanted to play. But now the ball was very close to her scary mouth.

I took a quick look around the desk and grabbed a small ruler. Using the ruler like a bat, I swung and hit the ball hard.

This time, the ball rolled much

farther away and Poppy chased after it.

I worked fast to loosen the string, but the pup came right back and set the ball on the desk again.

"WOOF-WOOF!" she barked.

Her shiny white teeth looked SHARP-SHARP-SHARP.

I picked up the ruler again and aimed it in a different direction.

I gave the ball an even harder whack. It flew off the desk and rolled under Richie's bed!

I heard Poppy's paws racing across the floor, but I didn't stop to watch her.

Instead, I stood up on my back

paws and gave the string a good tug with my front paws.

Then I gave the wheel a spin, and when the paper clip hit the bell, it rang.

DING-DING-DING!

It worked!

I raced back to my cage and closed the door behind me just as Poppy returned with the ball.

"Sorry, Poppy. I don't want to play fetch anymore," I squeaked.

Poppy just looked up at me, wagging her tail.

It wasn't long before Richie came back to his room.

"Get out, Poppy," he said as he shooed her out of the room.

"Richie! We're about to leave for school!" his dad called. "Get your project together."

"What's the point?" Richie said. "It doesn't work anyway."

"Try it!" I squeaked.

Richie walked over to the desk and looked down at my wheel. "I don't understand why it doesn't ring," he said.

Then he gave the wheel a spin
and the clip hit
the bell.

DING!

"I don't believe it," Richie said.
He spun the wheel again.

DING!

"It works!" Richie grinned,
giving the wheel another spin.

DING!

"I don't know what happened,"
he said. "But I'm glad it's fixed
now."

Richie wasn't the only one who was GLAD-GLAD-GLAD!

～～～

Once we got to school, Richie and all the other students in Room 26 set up their projects.

"Og, you're not going to believe what happened," I told my froggy friend.

"BOING-BOING!" he answered.

Og sounded concerned, so I said, "Don't worry. It turned out well in the end."

Then Mrs. Brisbane asked my friends to explain their science projects.

It was interesting to learn that plain water froze faster than sugar water. And Heidi said the salt water didn't freeze at all!

Sayeh showed us the beans she'd grown. The beans that had received the most light grew the best.

And the colorful mold that Gail had grown in her refrigerator was amazing!

Finally, it was Richie's turn.

He explained his experiment to the class. "Each time the wheel went around, the bell rang and I marked it down."

Then he pointed to the chart. "I had him spin for three minutes each time. I noticed that he slowed down toward the end of the experiment. So even hamsters get tired!"

Then he showed everyone how he did it. Richie took me out of my cage and placed me on my wheel.

"Why don't we all get a little closer so we can watch?" Mrs. Brisbane said.

I was HAPPY-HAPPY-HAPPY to start spinning.

DING-DING-DING!

The bell rang every single time the wheel went around.

DING-DING-DING-DING!

"Look at him go!" Lower-Your-Voice-A.J. shouted.

Golden-Miranda cheered me on, too. "Faster, Humphrey, faster!"

When three minutes were up, Richie stopped the wheel. "That's it, Humphrey," he said.

"You've done a wonderful job, Richie," Mrs. Brisbane said.

I looked up at Richie.

He had a huge smile on his face.

I think I had a huge smile on my face, too.

(Some humans think that hamsters don't smile, but we do.)

"Good job," Kirk told Richie. "But I still think you should have turned Humphrey into a monster!"

I like Kirk a lot, but I didn't agree with him.

I just want to be a helpful classroom hamster who goes home with my classmates on the weekend.

I love going home with my friends.

Even friends who have very playful puppies!